David Goes to School.

By David Shannon

THE BLUE SKY PRESS

An Imprint of Scholastic Inc. · New York

AUTHOR'S NOTE

A few years ago, my mother sent me a book I made when I was a little boy. The text consisted entirely of the words "no" and "David"—they were the only words I knew how to spell—and it was illustrated with drawings of David doing all sorts of things he wasn't supposed to do. I thought it would be fun to do a remake celebrating all the time-honored ways moms say "no." The new version was called *No, David!*

Well, David's in trouble again. This time it's his teacher saying, "No, David!" It seems that kids haven't changed much over the years, and neither have school rules, some of which date back even farther than the invention of sneakers.

Of course, "yes" is a wonderful word...but "yes" doesn't stop kids from running in the halls.

For Mrs. Harms, Miss Deffert, Mrs. Miller, Mr. Helpingstine,

Mr. Watson, Mrs. Williams, Mr. McDougal, and, of course, Heidi.

THE BLUE SKY PRESS

Copyright © 1999 by David Shannon   All rights reserved.

No part of this publication may be reproduced or stored in a retrieval system or transmitted in any form or by any means, electronic, mechanical, photocopying, recording, or otherwise, without written permission of the publisher.

For information regarding permission, please write to: Permissions Department,

The Blue Sky Press, an imprint of Scholastic Inc., 555 Broadway, New York, New York 10012.

The Blue Sky Press is a registered trademark of Scholastic Inc.

Library of Congress catalog card number: 98-50404   ISBN 0-590-48087-1

10 9 8 7 6 5 4   03 04 05 06 07

Printed in Singapore   46   First printing, August 1999

David's teacher always said...

NO, DAVID!

No yelling.
No pushing.
No running
in the halls.

Wait your

turn, David!

David!

Recess is over!

David, have

Yes, David...

You can go home now.